For Kelsey

Jim La Marche
02

ALBERT

DONNA JO NAPOLI

Illustrated by **Jim LaMarche**

SILVER WHISTLE • HARCOURT, INC. • *San Diego New York London*

Silver Whistle is a trademark of Harcourt, Inc., registered in the United States of America and/or other jurisdictions.

Library of Congress Cataloging-in-Publication Data
Napoli, Donna Jo, 1948–
Albert/Donna Jo Napoli; illustrated by Jim LaMarche—1st ed.
p. cm.
"Silver Whistle."
Summary: One day when Albert is at his window, two cardinals
come to build a nest in his hand, an event that changes his life.
ISBN 0-15-201572-8
[1. Birds—Fiction. 2. Birds—Nests—Fiction.] I. LaMarche, Jim, ill. II. Title.
PZ7.N15A1 2001
[E]—dc21   97-7089

C E G H F D
Printed in Singapore

The illustrations in this book were done in colored pencil on Arches watercolor paper.
The display type was set in Trio.
The text type was set in Cochin.
Printed and bound by Tien Wah Press, Singapore
This book was printed on totally chlorine-free Nymolla Matte Art paper.
Production supervision by Sandra Grebenar and Ginger Boyer
Designed by Linda Lockowitz

ALBERT SAT AT HIS TABLE and drank tomato juice and listened to the noises of the morning.

The people in the apartment above clattered downstairs and out the door on their way to work.

The dog next door barked hello to everyone who passed.

Children giggled on their way to school.

These were good noises.

Albert stood up and worked his hand out between the grillwork over the window. He wanted to check the weather.

The garbage truck rumbled by.

That wasn't a good noise.

Albert shook his head. "Too cold," he said. He shut the window and rubbed his hands to warm them.

Then he sat down and read the comic strip.

The next day Albert ate lunch and listened to the noises of midday.

The mailman sang as he slung his pack over his shoulder.

The snack vendor shouted out the day's special: golden bean cakes.

The flower lady laughed with her customers. Good noises today. Very good noises.

Albert went to the window and reached his hand toward the maple tree. How was the weather today?

Two men walked past arguing.

Now that wasn't a good noise.

"Too damp." Albert shut the window and wiped his hands on his trousers.

Then he took out a pack of cards and did card tricks.

The next day Albert said, "Too hot."

And the next day, "Too breezy."

Albert told himself that when the weather was right, just right, he'd put on his hat and go for a walk. And every day the weather seemed good at first. But after a moment more, it turned out the weather was never just right.

So Albert listened to baseball games on the radio and cut pictures out of magazines and wrote postcards he never mailed.

Then one sunny day, Albert stuck his hand out the
window, and the next thing he knew, a twig appeared in it.
Albert looked around in surprise. A cardinal flew by and
dropped in another twig. And then there were two cardinals,
a bright red male and a brown-yellow female, and both of
them were dropping twig after twig. Albert watched,
dumbfounded, as his now cupped hand filled to the brim.

The cardinals fluttered and fussed and poked and pulled.
They heaped grasses into the center of the twigs. Finally the
female shaped the nest to fit her breast and settled in.

Albert stared at her. "Umm, excuse me, but my arm's not a branch."

But the cardinal didn't even look at him. She flew off, leaving a nest of four tiny eggs in Albert's hand.

With his free hand, Albert scratched his head. If he pulled his arm in, twisting to get it back through the grillwork, the nest would surely fall apart.

So he stood there.

The mother cardinal returned.

Albert stood with his arm out the window. "Mrs. Cardinal, I think you picked a poor spot to build a nest."

But the cardinal just whistled and fell asleep.

That night Albert slept standing up.

The next day the mother cardinal kept the eggs warm, while the father cardinal fed her.

Albert rubbed his aching neck. "Listen, I hate to disappoint you two, but I'm not sure this is going to work."

The cardinals looked at Albert. Then they preened each other.

That night Albert slept standing up again.

The third day Albert rotated his shoulders to get the kinks out.

The mother bird flew to the ground and pecked at a grub.

Albert took a good look at the eggs for the first time: perfect sea blue ovals with red-brown spots.

The father bird flew down and chattered at the mother bird. She flew back to the eggs and sat on them.

"Pretty eggs," said Albert gently.

The cardinal gave a quizzical chirp.

Day after day Albert stood, the nest in his hand. He began each day by watching the birds. Then he looked around.

Once a plane roared overhead. Albert's first urge was to pull his arm in and shut the window. But the nest kept him there. So he watched the plane till it went out of sight, and soon he found himself dreaming about the places those passengers were going to visit. And he smiled.

Once a man and a woman came out of a building yelling. They turned their backs on each other, and both walked off in a huff. Albert wanted so much to pull his arm in and shut the window. But the nest was there. So he stayed put. About an hour later, the man appeared from one direction and the woman appeared from the other. Each held a wrapped present. They laughed and hugged.

Albert dreamed about what might be in those presents. And he smiled again.

Albert didn't only dream. Whenever the mother cardinal hopped off the nest, even for a moment, Albert breathed his hot breath onto the eggs to warm them.

And once when the mother cardinal was away, a cat walked along the ledge beneath Albert's arm. It flicked its tail and looked up curiously. It crouched, ready to spring.

Albert screeched.

The cat ran off.

Albert chuckled.

A week passed, and one morning when Albert opened his mouth, he peeped. The father cardinal looked at him askance. But Albert peeped insistently.

The cardinal flew off. He returned with a beetle.

Albert wrinkled his nose and jerked his head away.

The cardinal ate the beetle. Then he flew off again. This time he returned with a blackberry.

Albert ate it gratefully.

From that day on, Albert peeped and the father cardinal fed him blackberries. And Albert smiled at the noises all around him.

Days passed.

On the twelfth morning, Albert spied a crack in one of the eggs. He put his face to the grillwork so he could see everything perfectly.

The second egg cracked.

And the third.

And the fourth.

The baby birds pecked their way out, wet and scraggly.

"Good work." Albert smiled. "Welcome."

In the next few weeks, the mother and father cardinals fed their brood, including Albert, who learned to love seeds and berries and even, eventually, beetles. The mother sat on Albert's wrist and sang her joy. The father flew to the top of the maple and sang his pride.

The parents whistled to the fledglings, encouraging them to test their wings.

Soon the first fledgling left the nest.

Then the second.

Then the third.

But one stayed. He hopped up Albert's arm and pecked at his nose. He looked worriedly at the ground.

"Go for it, Birdie," said Albert. "Fly."

The fledgling looked down again. He kept his wings close to his body.

Albert stuck out his hat in front of the fledgling. "Come on," he said. "Give it a try."

The fledgling jumped into the hat.

Albert tossed him up lightly.

He fluttered a little and landed safely back in the hat with a peep.

Albert tossed him higher.

He fluttered a lot and landed back in the hat with a loud chirp.

Albert tossed him high high high.

The fledgling looked around and spread his wings. He flew to the maple tree and whistled.

Albert smiled and whistled back.

The nest sat empty in Albert's hand.

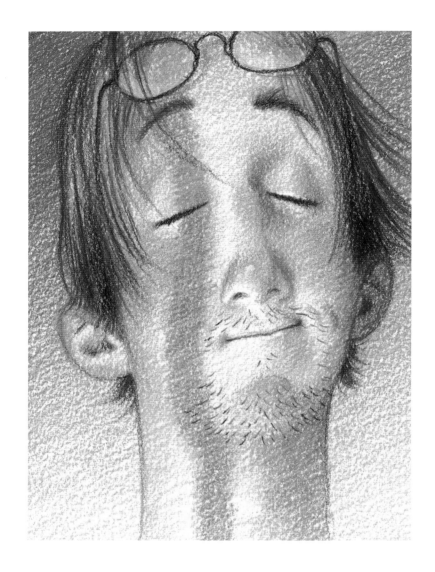

He drew his arm in through the grillwork and the nest fell.
Albert looked at the grass and the trees and the sky. He
listened to laughter nearby, a good noise, and the siren of an
ambulance far off, a bad noise. And Albert knew now that
both were part of this big, wonderful world. He put his face
up to the grillwork and felt the wind and the sun on his
cheeks. "Just right," he said.

Albert smoothed his hair and brushed off his hat. After so
long, he hardly looked himself. He went outside for a walk.

Now Albert walks often. And sometimes, just sometimes, when no one's looking, he flies.